MISTLETOE AND THE GRINCHY BILLIONAIRE

Second Chance Small Town Romance

BARBI COX

ONE

Hayden

I RIDE BACK INTO MY SLEEPY HOMETOWN, HATING THE SNOW already. Being up north keeps me from riding my Harley, and the cold temperatures have everyone bundled up against the snow. Not that I can blame them, but in Miami, it's still warm enough to show some cleavage and leg. I already miss the added scenery.

"Right here," I say to the driver as I stare at the *one* hotel in the whole town.

"It looks like a magical place, sir," my driver comments.

"Yeah, belongs right in a snow globe," I scoff.

The driver unloads my stuff as I ignore the cold getting under my leather jacket and sweater. I know I'll be fine once I'm inside. If my mother hadn't dragged me up here because my sister's pregnant, I'd still be plenty warm. Taking a deep breath, I fight the urge to have a smoke. It will keep me outside longer and considering how small the town is, someone might notice me and then I'll have to deal with plenty.

"Is that all, sir?" the driver asks.

"Yup, just the two bags. I'm not planning on staying long," I say.

He nods and I head into the hotel. I'm dying to rip these layers off me. I feel even more naked with all my tattoos covered. A suit in the office is one thing, but a fuzzy sweater on top of jeans and my jacket is beyond intolerable. I get the key to my room, head to the 'best suite', which is the only room that has a bedroom separate from the living area, and flop on the bed after ripping off my clothes.

Stretching over the bed, I hold my arms up, smiling at my tattoos.

After a shower and tossing some of my clothes around the room, I feel better. I crack the window, ignoring the fact that I'm only in a towel and light a cigarette, ignoring the 'no smoking' warning. I've got more money than I can count. I don't need to worry about some petty fee of $250.

Let them fine me. I could buy the whole damn hotel.

I look over the main street and remember ruling it with some friends. They considered us the 'bad kids', which meant shop owners hated us since we stole, parents would do anything to keep their kids away, and the girls couldn't get enough.

Not that we ever gave them more than one go except for the ones that lived to please. I notice some teenager walking down Main Street in leggings, an oversized sweater, and one of those knitted hats with a pompom on top.

My lips turn up.

The only girl I didn't even get a kiss from–Molly Moore. I used to joke that she would taste like M&M's because of her name, but I still remember her honey-blonde hair, her budding curves, and her perpetual goodness. She gave everyone a smile sweeter than candy, lived for Christmas and charity work, and never hesitated to be sweet even to us, no matter how much we flirted.

She was smart, sexy, and sweet. On top of that, she was impossible to snag for even a kiss - always flitting from event to event. I saw her put her foot down when one of my friends tried to distract her for long enough to set up a date. Tommy had walked away, promising us he'd get her to go out with him while we'd just cackled.

After I finish my smoke and shut the window, I lie back on my bed, thinking about the delicious Molly, the girl we all wanted but none of us got. Is she still here? Still perfect? No, she was meant for more than small-town life, not that she'd complain about living here forever.

She loves Mistletoe Meadows.

I bet she's developed in the last ten years, but I'm sure her sapphire eyes are just as beautiful, her voice just as sweet, and her curiosity is still as intense. The corner of my mouth lifts as I feel myself harden.

She'd give me a thorough once over, note all my new tattoos, and suck her full bottom lip. She'd look at me from under her lashes, move close, and tell me she waited just for me, that she missed me, that I'm all she's been waiting for and more.

I stroke over my cock, closing my eyes as I imagine her walking in, blushing, then taking over. She'd use her delicate fingers first, wrapping them around me, then she'd beg for a taste.

Fuck, I can picture her hot, wet mouth sliding around me, struggling to take every inch until she moans around me. Moaning softly, I lift my hips, imagining myself grabbing her hair and showing her how a good girl takes cock. She'll need a lesson considering how sweet she is. I can teach her how to be dirty. I stroke myself faster, thinking of her gorgeous face, those curves.

"Show me how good you can be. What a good girl you are," I growl, my voice low and throaty.

I tighten my hand around the head of my cock, then stoke down again, feeling the vein that presses against the side as my palm moves across it. I grit my teeth to keep myself quiet, but even the fantasy of Molly is so intense, I can't stand it. She's been my naughty thought for years, the one who got away because I wasn't refined enough to have her. I wasn't good enough, but I'd love to put her down on her knees, to see her choking on my dick after seeing everything I've become despite what people have thought about me.

I'd grip her hair, make her look at me as I fuck her mouth, bend her to every order until she's eager to make me come before I ever fill her with my fingers or cock. Picturing her begging for my dick, squirming as I fill her throat, using her tongue and mouth until I'm spiraling pushes me over the edge so I finish in my palm.

Sighing, I enjoy the satisfaction of a quick release until I clean myself up, pull on boxers and fleece pajama pants. Going back to the window, I look at how decorated the city is. Giant Christmas ornaments hang from street lights. There are Christmas lights hanging from every awning. Most of the shops have snowmen, Santa, reindeer, or presents drawn on their windows, not to mention the giant Christmas Tree at the one round about on Main Street. It's not lit yet. That ceremony is in a few days.

My phone dings, distracting me.

Work never stops and nothing can happen without the boss. The only question is—which side of work is calling? The legal side or the less legal side. I check my personal phone first and see nothing.

Grabbing my business phone, I put it to my ear just for Marissa, my assistant, to talk. "Mr. Grant, there are people here who want to see you and say they have a meeting with you. I told them you're not in the state, but-"

"Who?" I ask.

There's a muffled conversation, then a quick answer. "Mr. Duncan?"

"Ah, they were supposed to meet with me this morning and didn't show. Tell them I've moved on and if they want anything from me, they'll have to wait until after Christmas," I say.

"Sir ..." she hesitates.

"Or pass the phone, Marissa," I growl, already out of patience. Some assistant she is. She doesn't have any backbone to stand up to even low-level clients.

"Listen here, I emailed requesting-"

"You requested a change of time ten minutes after you were supposed to be at my office," I say.

"I had a business emergency and-"

"I don't care," I pick at my clean nails. "It's not *my* responsibility to get you to show up on time. So, if you still want to be partners, you'll meet when it's convenient for me and I'll be making over fifty percent off this deal."

"You can't just change things!" he barks. "There's no way anyone on the board will agree to this!"

"That sounds like another 'you' problem, doesn't it? You need my land and my connections. They don't come for free and since you don't respect my time, I can find someone who will. Happy holidays," I sneer before hanging up.

I let him stew for a few minutes, then call my assistant back. She picks up. "Mr. Grant!"

"I'm not to be contacted for anything less than a fire being set in the building or murder. I'll contact *you* when that changes."

"Yes, sir," she whimpers.

"If they don't leave, have security throw them out," I say before hanging up again.

Being CEO was supposed to be a nothing job, not a huge amount of work. That's why I took on the role of the boss at a motorcycle club. I loved being in the club and having a special place for my talents at evading the law, getting places I'm not supposed to, and ordering others around while on top of the food chain. Instead, I'm doing double the amount of work and not getting the same amount of freedom as promised.

After checking in with the guys of my M.C., I set up an auto-response for my email so I'm not bothered, then hold my personal phone. I should text my mother.

One look in the mirror makes me drop my phone. It can wait until tomorrow when I feel like getting dressed. I run my hand over my washboard abs and smile at the tattoos on my body. It's a mix of traditional Japanese work alongside black and gray demons and skulls. A fun, unacceptable combination in the eyes of business and my family.

I'll wait until tomorrow to be the son my mother wishes I was for a few hours before escaping to whatever bar in town is open.

That's what I do. I have a late breakfast, early lunch with my parents, keeping my tattoos covered by my coat and smiling through conversations while keeping half my life a secret. My mother talks about how much I've cleaned up, how happy she is that I turned my life around and she can call me successful at twenty-nine until I'm worried I'm going to break my jaw by clenching it so hard.

A part of me wants my parents to be proud of me, but more for what I've done with myself, not some business that was far too easy to work up through by ass kissing, manipulation, and stealing assignments from other people.

"I'll be back tomorrow, when Lisa and John are here," I promise, referencing my perfect sister and her husband.

My mom tries to ask me more while she keeps gushing about me being a success and becoming a billionaire when they were so worried that I'd end up in juvie. She keeps talking until my dad walks me outside, as quiet as ever. He glances at the car I rented this morning. He grunts once, a sound of approval, and that's the most I get out of him other than his normal greeting—a handshake that squeezes a bit too hard.

I count the seconds until I can leave and head to a bar in town. Even when I walk in, inhaling the scent of wood and a semi-dusty heater, I only feel sane after downing a whole beer. I remove my jacket to reveal my arms, then stretch and sigh once.

"Is that you, Hayden?" A masculine voice asks.

I look over and see my old friend Tommy. I grin, shake his hand, and see a wedding band around his finger. Things do change. "Who's the lucky woman?"

Just as he opens his mouth to answer, the woman of my fantasies walks in. Her honey-blonde hair curls just below her very full breasts. Her wide hips have filled out just like I imagined, and now she's a woman in every single way imaginable. Still, she's got those gorgeous full lips, shining sapphire eyes, and just like when we were teens, her cheeks and nose are pink thanks to the cold.

She takes off her jacket, showing off some cleavage, and I almost groan out loud.

"Tommy," she greets him, rubbing his arm. I look at her finger, assuming the worst, but there's no ring, not an engagement ring, a promise ring, or a wedding band. Her eyes meet mine and her lips part as she gives me a long once-over. "Hayden?"

TWO

Molly

———

There's no way I'm staring at Hayden Grant. It's not
possible. He's been gone for a little over ten years and now
he's standing right here after flipping off the town while
guiding his motorcycle with sheer luck.

He swore he'd never come back, and I'm tempted to
believe this isn't him. But his black hair has the same unruly
curls even if he has it organized and slicked back, there's a
rebellious curl dipping into his hazel eyes. His olive skin tone,
his familiar sharp jaw, the scruff he swore he'd never shave, I
even see the little scar from the nose ring he used to have
along with the scar through his eyebrow that he got when he
fell off a dirt bike.

Sure, he has double the tattoos and double the muscle and
maybe he's gotten a little taller, but it's Hayden Grant, the
menace of society back during his least favorite time of year.

All I can do is stare up at him. My lips part as my brain
tries to restart. I'd made peace with never seeing him again,
but here he is. The man who had me looking up "how to flirt"
when I was fifteen, acting as if I had never seen a guy before.

Tommy elbows me. "I heard my assignment. Don't worry.
I can get sparklers for the celebration."

"Thanks," I say, blinking myself back to the present and grinning at Tommy. "Tell Debbie I said hi."

"I swear you see my wife more than I do," Tommy chuckles. "Thanks for the cookies, by the way."

"It's been a long time. We should catch up; stay, have a drink," Hayden interjects.

"Oh no, Molly's got a to-do list a mile long. Apparently, she's more than just a genius with architecture," Tommy teases, poking my nose.

I swat at his hand. "Stop it."

"See, nothing's changed. She still doesn't have time for fun," he snorts before going over to a group of guys.

I fight the urge to stick my tongue out at him

"You know, rushing around isn't good for you. Can you spare five minutes for an old friend?" Hayden asks, as he gives me that trademark lopsided smile. It's always naughty and tempting, even if it looks wrong without a cigarette between his teeth. "Is it me? I don't bite unless I'm asked to."

It's unfair that my body still reacts to his teasing the same way. All it takes is that smile and a bit of innuendo to have me heated to the point I don't need long sleeves. I clear my throat. "One beer."

"How gracious."

I roll my eyes. We're not the same people. I've looked him up once or twice. He's a CEO of a billion dollar company now, even if he's still mysterious. No one knows much about his personal life other than he's never seen with the same woman twice—which is a reminder from when we were teens.

He'd always have a smile ready for me along with some teasing words, but there'd always be some other girl, older, hotter, on his arm. Hayden motions for me to sit beside him and I clear my throat as I join and ask for a holiday cider.

"So, you're back?" I ask, trying to be cool and calm. "How long can a billionaire escape his business?"

"Are you asking if I'm going to ruin your wholesome Christmas?" he chuckles.

"No, I'm just surprised you're here, that's all. And that you remember me," I say, smiling because I can't help myself.

"How could I forget the sweetest girl in high school?" he asks.

"How could you remember me when there were always others hanging around? Tommy and your gang, the ..." I don't want to sound jealous. "And it's been ten years. Life has changed plenty."

"You haven't forgotten me either. I saw that once-over. Am I still in your naughty thoughts?" he asks, making me choke on my drink. Hayden rubs my back. "Easy, I was kidding, Molly."

"You weren't," I only reply to his last sentence.

"Don't you know? Everything I say is either eighty percent kidding or some kind of bullshit," he says.

I calm my coughing and fan my face. I'd wanted Hayden plenty as a silly teenager, but I realized how bad that would have been for me. He was a gateway drug. One kiss from Hayden and I could have ended up with a cigarette in my mouth. From there, I could have dressed in leather, climbing on the back of motorcycles for the thrill, skipping school, having sex, going to parties, drinking, I could have derailed myself because he's the person that's too easy to get lost in.

And I'm happy as I am. If I give an inch with Hayden, he'll take it all for as long as he wants it, then leave me in the dust when he rides out of here, flipping off the town he never wanted to be in.

Which is why it doesn't matter that I've googled him every time he didn't come to a reunion (why not have them yearly instead of every decade), or whenever something made me think of him. I'm doing things with my life, devoting it to my goals, and Hayden has some kind of demonic power to ruin everything that matters and replace it with him.

I take another long drink. "So, what have you been up to?"

"You must be the only one who doesn't know," he scoffs. "I'm sure my mom gushes about it."

"I'm sure she does to people she talks to," I say, as if I haven't eavesdropped more than once as she gushes about the vacation home he bought them or how he paid off all their debt, or when he made his first million.

"I'm C.E.O. of Venetian Trust–a trading company. It's pretty boring, more work than it's supposed to be for a C.E.O., which means I need better assistants, I guess."

"Not being paid to breathe?"

"Not yet. Means I need to do something about that, huh?" he says before tapping the bar twice and ordering two shots of whiskey. "I hear–that you're an architect?"

"I am."

"I thought you'd be an artist."

"I put my art skills to good use. I love designing buildings," I say with a smile.

"Something tells me that's not all you do. Are you running all the big festivals and events here now?" he asks.

I want to tell him no, just to prove he doesn't know everything, but he's not wrong. So instead, I finish my drink and grab my purse. I pull out my card, ready to leave, but Hayden shakes his head. "You're not paying. Do the shot I ordered to keep you warm."

Is this his version of flirting now? Being light and breezy? No. Why does it matter anyway? He doesn't like me. He doesn't *like* anyone. He likes playing with people. That's it. I down the shot to prove I can, and he grins at me, looking me over again.

"I might not be here for long, but I would love to catch up with you, Molly. My suite has a fireplace. If I remember right, you like smores."

"Hayden, we barely know each other. I reminded you to

return library books, and you destroyed them. I'd get excited about Christmas and you'd try to ruin it like the Grinch. Let's not pretend there's anything we need to say to each other." I sigh.

"What happened to your sunny nature? You used to give me your sweetest smiles and always tell me to be safe. Many people thought you had a crush on me," he says, as if it's a secret.

I just stare at him. I shake my head. "You're serious."

"I was one of the people who thought that, sweetheart," he growls, no smile, no teasing, just his intense hazel eyes gazing into mine until I'm tempted to find every trace of green in his irises.

"Even if I did, that was ten years ago. People change, get smarter, realize that they were wrong and silly," I answer with a shrug.

He considers that. I paste on the smile he's so eager for. "Merry Christmas, Hayden."

"Bah, humbug," he snorts.

I don't get his vendetta against Christmas or against our town or society. He's not a teenager anymore. He's thirty, and he's the same person; covering up any bit of actual emotion with a bad-boy smirk, an insult, or some show to prove he's too much 'man' for emotions.

Later that night, I meet up with my three best friends. We've been close since high school, despite some time apart. Sitting in Angela's coffee and sweets shop, the four of us take up two of the couches set out. Angela keeps glancing out the door, smoothing out her lovely brown hair. Tamsin nurses her iced latte, although it's freezing outside and my cousin Charlotte keeps picking at her nails.

"I love Christmas," I say, despite wanting to tell the girls that Hayden is back in town.

"It makes so much work." Angela sighs. "I mean, I love how sweet most people are, but the orders are near constant and I feel like I have no time. It's nowhere near as magical as when we were kids."

"It could be." Charlotte sighs. "If it was like the movies I love where romance happens before Christmas morning."

"Really? That's where you're going with this?" Tamsin rolls her eyes. "There are more important things than guys."

"Yeah, but that doesn't mean a life without guys is as comfortable, right Molly?" Charlotte asks before shaking her head. "Sorry, asking the wrong person."

"Who's the right person to ask?" Angela grumbles. "We're all single."

"I'm happily between partners," Tamsin scoffs. "Leave me out of it."

"Still, Christmas makes me want someone to cuddle," Angela admits. "I mean, Lottie's right. It could be so romantic. Curling up by the fire with someone. Ice skating, going to the winter festival, kissing under the mistletoe."

"Proving to my family that I *can* get a boyfriend," Charlotte sighs.

I bite my bottom lip. "As if any of us have the time, though, right?"

"You make time for love, otherwise it happens anyway," Charlotte says. "I wish there was a star for us to wish on."

"Wouldn't that count as your wish?" Tamsin asks.

"No!"

We all laugh and talk about the festival before I let it slip that Hayden's back in town. Tamsin stares at me, her mouth full of a cookie. She forces it down, so she doesn't look like a chipmunk, and clears her throat. "How do you feel about that, Molly?"

"Don't start with that," I groan.

"Look!" Charlotte interrupts, pointing out the window.

We gather around to see a shooting star across the clear sky. No snow tonight. I smile, but Charlotte giggles. "We all have a wish."

"We're not kids," Tamsin argues.

"So it won't hurt anything if we make a wish. At best it comes true, at worse, we can laugh about it later," she argues. "I wish for a good man, a partner that matches me, someone I can bring home for Christmas."

Angela sighs. "I wish I'd run into my ex-boyfriend. I think we could rekindle things."

I bite my bottom lip. "I wish the one who got away would be the one I thought he could be."

Tamsin groans. "I wish to have more than my cat to cuddle."

We all tease Tamsin. Tamsin, who's cold as ice, from her white-blonde hair, pale blue eyes, and snowy white skin, has a soft side, I'm sure of it. Maybe having someone other than her cat to cuddle would soften her prickly side. She points at me.

"So I get made fun of, but Molly, who's obviously talking about Hayden, doesn't get any shit at all?"

"I don't mean Hayden," I lie.

"Bullshit," Angela laughs, spilling her coffee. "You mooned over him and pouted for a week after he left. Now he's back and-"

"And I left him alone at a bar after having one drink and a shot. It was barely a conversation. He hasn't grown up at all," I say, defending myself.

"But you want him to," Charlotte hugs me. "I hope your wish comes true, Molly. You deserve someone who appreciates your ambition."

Despite every word out of my mouth, refusing to admit I want Hayden, I keep my fingers crossed behind my back. I do want him to grow up and feel comfortable sharing himself with the world.

THREE

Hayden

BEING HERE IS AS BORING AS I REMEMBER. I WENT HOME FOR dinner, was who I'm expected to be with a little bit of edge, and was told its time to wind down at seven. Seven! I wander through town, seeing couples everywhere with or without kids. I shake my head.

I don't get the allure of quiet living. There's so much in life to experience, but half the world seems willing to ignore it. The other half 'grows out of it' as if living is only for the young. I want to travel, I want to experience everything. I'll only 'settle down' when there's a reason to.

I hold to that until the next afternoon when I end up at the skating rink. I remember kissing plenty of girls under the bridge, so I head over there. When I stand at the peak, looking out at all the people skating, someone bumps me.

Looking over, I find Molly chained to a white fluffy dog. I stare at it, then her. The dog sniffs my leg and sits, wagging its tail until I give in and pat its head.

"We've talked about stranger danger, Teddy," Molly says. "Oh ..."

"Well, according to you, I am a stranger, so," I say.

Molly looks up at me for a long moment. The only sound

is her dog's tail moving in the snow. She sighs. "I wasn't fair yesterday. I'm sorry."

"Are you?"

"Not really. You come on very strong," she admits with a soft smile. She banishes it. "But you haven't changed and since you're still the same as you were when you were nineteen-"

"Am I? Are you sure I'm not worse? Better? It's not like we had a full conversation at the bar," I mumble.

She arches her eyebrow. "So you just make bad first impressions?"

"You're not as nice as I remember," I grunt, leaning over the railing to look at the skaters. "Do you still skate?"

Silence greets me at first, but then she sighs. "I haven't in a solid three years."

I swallow. "You're a wonderful skater. Made me want to learn for a while."

"Why didn't you?"

"I was doing other things," I answer, though I'm not about to list off all the things I vandalized or places I broke into. "Everyone here skates. When everyone does something because it's tradition or expected, the magic is gone."

"You could still learn."

"Why?"

"Because you might enjoy it. Plus, it's something you haven't done. How do you know you won't enjoy it?" Molly asks, no venom, just a genuine question.

"When did you get your dog?" I ask instead, avoiding how right she is.

"Teddy? It'll be a year on Christmas. He was a present last year," she answers with a smile. "My own living teddy bear. But don't let his cute face fool you. He has to be extra adorable to make up for all the shedding I'll deal with in winter."

I chuckle as the dog jumps up between us, his big paws on the railing. My eyes flit to Molly and her eyes meet mine.

There's less hostility today, more of the blatant curiosity I remember. She watches me from under her lashes, steadily fueling fantasies I'll put to use later as she sucks her bottom lip and looks away, cheeks flushed.

"Why did you come back, Hayden?"

"My sister's pregnant and supposed to have her kid soon. She wanted all the family here for her baby's first Christmas. She's sure her son will be here by Christmas Eve," I sigh. "Apparently, me saying he won't remember either way doesn't fly."

"You are a Grinch," Molly murmurs. "Someone needs to show you why Christmas is fun."

"Let me guess, you're talking about time off, presents, parties, Christmas movies, snow? Did I leave out corporate greed and manipulative advertising? I should have said those first. I use them in my marketing," I say before snapping my fingers.

Molly narrows her eyes at me, then looks at my hands. She rolls her eyes and pulls gloves out of her pocket. They're bright pink with snowmen on them. I stare at her, then the gloves. "What?"

"Your hands are turning blue. Put these on."

"I'd rather have frostbite."

"Please, Hayden?" she asks.

Before I can stop myself, I grab the gloves and pull them on. They're too small, don't even cover the heel of my hands, but my fingers are warm. Molly nods once. "I made them for Tamsin, but I can always make her new ones."

"You're taking these back. They don't fit," I huff.

"I'm sure they destroy your bad boy image," she agrees. "But your list is wrong about Christmas."

"Is it?"

"I love the festivities like the winter festival. I love baking cookies with people you love, which I guess is because they have time off work. I enjoy making presents for people, thinking of how much I've enjoyed time with them over the year. I love spending time with family, decorating my tree, making snowmen ... so many things that I don't get to do as much anymore," she says.

We stand in silence for a while. How can Molly make me feel like a dick so easily? Not just a dick either, a cynical, stupid dick. I close my eyes for a long moment and clear my throat. "You used to be nice."

"Yeah, I know."

"If there's any of that nice-ness left, you should meet me here later tonight."

"Why would I do that?"

"To teach me how to fucking skate," I huff before petting her dog. "And bring the bear. I like him."

"He can't skate," she argues.

"Yeah, which means he won't laugh at me when I fall on my ass," I grumble.

I see the ghost of a smile on Molly's lips. "Seven thirty. They close at eight-thirty."

"Then we'll meet at eight-fifteen and I'll show you how far my charm can go," I barter.

She gives me a disapproving look and I groan. "How much trouble can I get into when you're Miss Responsible? We'll just stay a little after hours. It's not like they lock the rink up."

She points at me. "This is the only rule we'll be breaking and only because I own my own skates."

"Unless you get a rush from staying out late. Then I'll have to show you the very few fun places in town ... if they still exist," I tease.

"Don't push it. I'm close to changing my mind, Hayden," she warns me.

"I think you're going to show up."

"What's that?"

"You're curious," I chuckle. "I remember you always chasing anything that sparked your curiosity."

Molly takes a slow breath, closing her eyes as Teddy pushes off the railing and looks up at Molly, standing like a normal dog again. He cocks his head to the side as she closes her eyes and exhales heavily. "I'm going because I know you're going to say no to all the protective padding and I'm going to get to see you fall on your butt."

"I'll even let you kiss it better if you keep from laughing."

"Keep dreaming," Molly says before continuing on her walk. "Come on, Teddy. I don't want your paws freezing. Let's get back to the car."

After standing a bit longer in the snow, watching people put on fake smiles, seeing kids cry about how cold they are and seeing the reality of winter beyond the happy-Christmas fog, I head back to the hotel and get through a shower, jerking off again while thinking of Molly, then pull on jeans, a black turtleneck, and my leather jacket. I leave my hair free and wild, then stare at the stupid pink gloves she gave me for a day. I need to give them back. They're for someone else.

I grab my own black gloves and shove them in my coat pocket. I'll be plenty warm once we skate. I'm sure of that. Time and time again, I've said I want to do everything without thinking that there were things I hadn't done here. Of course, it would be Molly who points that out.

Stuffing the pink gloves in my pocket, I head to a restaurant to eat alone, then head to the skating rink at eight-fifteen. I rent skates despite the older woman glowering at me. I don't blame her. She's the principal we had in high school.

I give Mrs. Daily my most charming smile. "I'm meeting with Molly Moore and you know how she is."

Mrs. Daily almost scoffs when I hear someone crunching through the snow, stopping next to me. Mrs. Daily gives me a ticket, while staring at Molly in bewildered shock. Molly has her own skates and puts them on. I hand her the pink gloves as I show her my black ones.

"I prepared. Give these as a gift," I say.

She smiles and stuffs them in her coat pocket. "Thank you, Hayden. I didn't think you'd show."

"Why wouldn't I? It's my idea. You didn't bring Teddy, though. You realize he was the only thing keeping this from being a date," I point out.

"Very funny. It's not a date. Skating never is with a newbie," she teases as she laces her skates.

I slide out of my boots and shove my feet into the skates. I try to tighten them but have some trouble. It should be as simple as tying my shoes, but I have to hook the laces around pieces that go up over my ankle. It's frustrating as hell.

Molly gets on her knees in front of me and bats my hands out of the way to do it herself. She does it with flawless efficiency. Still, I just stare at her after shoving my foot in the other skate. If someone told me Molly would be on her knees in front of me, I'd have laughed.

She seems to realize her position at the same time, staring up at me as her face turns bright pink. "Don't say a word or I'll tie your laces together."

"Sure, sure. As long as you're-"

"That's enough words!" She exclaims, her voice pitching up.

I smirk and pull at her hair in the bun, pulling some locks free, so it's more like a ponytail by the time she finishes with my skates. She pushes herself up like she doesn't have literal blades strapped to her feet, then offers me her gloved hands. "Lesson one—stand."

We get through that lesson as I walk to the ice. I stare at it as she moves. This seems so much more dangerous than bungee jumping. Molly still tugs me onto the ice. I don't want to move my legs, try to keep them the right distance apart. Just let her tug me along. She laughs.

"You look terrified, Hayden."

"I'm not eager to fall. Ice is hard," I huff.

"I thought you were a big powerful man afraid of nothing. Where's all your charm and skill?" she teases me.

I hold her hands tighter, move my feet, and almost immediately, slip and drag Molly down with me as I fall on my back. Molly falls on top of me, our hands still linked. We stare at each other, our breath puffing out in visible plumes of fog until I crack a smile. Molly laughs and I join in despite the pain spreading down my back and ass.

"Isn't there something about teaching old dogs new tricks?" I groan as she pulls me up.

"Nope. We're doing this until all the lights go out," she decides.

"When's that?"

"Whenever I decide. I know where the breaker is," she giggles.

I groan, but let her keep teaching me. She laughs at me anytime I waver, fall, or grab onto her little self for stability, but I don't mind. Her laughing at me is a lot better than her hissing at me.

When I skate—even if I hate the idea of someone seeing me move like a newbie—she leads me under the bridge. I stop her there and stare at her. She seems to realize the make-out spot when she looks away, her cheeks red.

I lean down and kiss her cheek. "I could learn to like ice skating, Molly."

"You could learn to like plenty if you give it a chance," she counters with a smile.

I stare down at her until she bites her bottom lip, and I nod. "I will not disagree with that."

FOUR

Molly

Hayden keeps looking at me like he just wants to learn about me, even once we're off our skates and getting hot chocolate. He doesn't flinch when he takes a scalding sip of his drink. We're not the only ones in the shop. We're off in the corner, away from the crowds.

"I thought you'd want to start some kind of party here," I comment, desperate to break the silence.

"I thought you'd run away the second you turned off the lights at the skating rink," he counters.

I should have, but my wits ran off with any traces of logic after he called our hang-out session a date. I clear my throat. "You can't skate and not have hot chocolate."

"I've heard it's possible."

"And I've heard you're a recluse," I snap back.

He chuckles. "You're nowhere near as sunny as I remember, Molly."

"Life happens to everyone," I grumble.

"You say that like you're not an active participant in your life," he muses.

I reach forward and brush away the foam mustache clinging to his face. Hayden watches me, then takes my hand

and sucks my finger between his lips. I stare at him, frozen in place as his warm tongue flicks across the tip of my finger. He sucks again before releasing me.

"There's the innocent girl I knew once," he comments before taking another drink.

"Why ..." I trail off.

"Because I wanted to. I was also pretty sure I'd get away with it. I'm doubting my ability to drag your chair over here and seeing if peppermint tastes good in hot chocolate without half the people here noticing," he answers.

I slide him my cup and he smirks. "We both know that's not what I meant."

I clear my throat. "So ... you're here until Christmas?"

"And a few days after. Flights are insane, but I'll be back in Miami before the New Year."

So there's no reason to start anything with him. He'll leave, just like I assumed earlier.

"Don't tell me you'll miss me," he snorts.

"I won't," I promise him.

Hayden watches me again, his intense gaze on my face before he dips to my cleavage. It had been stupid to wear this winter dress. One that has a little peekaboo to show off some cleavage. I pulled on fleece-lined leggings to complete the look. Black dress, skin-colored leggings ... some part of me still wants him to want me. It's stupid. I'm not the girl that has flings. Even if I was, Hayden would ruin me.

He sighs. "Finish your drink so we can walk or something."

"Getting restless?"

"I don't enjoy wasting time and this feels like wasting time."

"You know you'll miss out on more things if you're always worried about what to do next," I say, warning him. "There are things happening right in front of you all the time."

He smirks and leans forward, his fiery gaze on me again.

"Is that so? Then what's happening right in front of me? Are you falling for me? Angling to get me under some mistletoe? Figuring out how to take me back to your place without everyone in town knowing?"

My mouth opens and closes. "N-no!"

"I would like to see Teddy again. I think he approves of me. Plus, he seems warm."

"If you're cold ..." Why is cuddling him under a blanket in front of a fireplace suddenly the only thing on my mind? Kissing him, finding out if he tastes like hot chocolate or something more like sin ... that seems like a good way to end the night. I banish the thought. "You should get a heavier coat."

He rolls his eyes. "Needing this many layers is reason enough to stay in Florida."

"But you don't get seasons there."

"Sure you do. There's winter, aka no swimming season, then there's allergy seasons, summer, hurricane season, love bug season, and an entire week of fall," he dismisses. "We know it's winter when iguanas fall out of trees."

I gape at him, then laugh. I can't help it. Hayden chuckles, too. "I wish I was kidding."

"That sounds horrific."

"The iguanas don't die, it's just the shock of cold paralyzing them if that helps," he says.

"It doesn't help," I insist.

We keep arguing about which is better, Florida or Mistletoe Meadows, but I sit taller. "You came back to Mistletoe Meadows. I've never been to Florida. That's winning enough."

"I will say Mistletoe Meadows has *one* redeeming quality—something you can't find anywhere else in the world," he murmurs, his voice softening as he looks me over.

"Don't start flirting again," I moan.

"Don't pretend you don't love it. I know that you have the hots for me," he teases, wiggling his eyebrows.

"You wouldn't know what to do with me."

"Oh, I have several ideas, honey," he promises me, his voice a low growl.

My face heats and I look away, taking a long drink to calm down. He's not allowed to be so attractive *and* an asshole.

"Tell me something real about you, Hayden. Something other people don't know or wouldn't guess."

He considers that for a moment. "I have a lock-picking kit."

I sigh.

Shaking his head, Hayden tries again. "I don't like being around my family."

"Really?"

He shrugs. "They expect the worst from me. Now that I'm CEO of a fortune 100 company my father doesn't say a word to me. My mother just gushes, calling me her CEO son as if I'm proud of it."

"Aren't you?"

"No. It was easy to get," he dismisses.

"Then what are you proud of?"

"Things I can't say in public." There's no sexual undercurrent in his voice and I don't want to be out in public for much longer. I know the temperature is going to dip, and I've noticed more than a few people whispering and looking over at us.

"You want to see Teddy?" I ask.

He blinks in surprise. "Yes. I like dogs."

"Finish up and we'll go."

"You want to show me your house?" His eyebrow raises in surprise.

"You'll be blown away," I chuckle.

We finish our drinks and I guide him to my car. He watches

as I adjust the seat a little, then forces the passenger seat almost all the way back. We head to my house and when I stop in front of the cottage-just out of town, Hayden stares, open-mouthed. I enjoy showing off what I'm capable of and my house is an example of that. It's a modernized cabin. Two stories (though the second floor is a loft with my bedroom and a bathroom rather than a whole floor), with windows that look out over the woods and show the mountains at sunset. The wrap around balcony has an overhang to keep the snow off and the inside is an open concept, to make the home feel bigger. It's raised from the ground and already lit up since we're in the driveway.

"Holy shit, Molly," he breathes.

"I'm a talented architect," I say.

He chuckles. "I fucking see that."

When we get inside, I take off my shoes and spread my feet over the hardwood. I have heated floors throughout the house. It was a necessary luxury. I also have the lights set up to be motion activated after ten p.m., so I don't trip on my half-asleep ventures to get water.

Teddy runs up to us, turning in circles. Hayden scratches his ears. "I'll take him out since your shoes are off."

He follows through, telling Teddy all about how he's prettier than snow and much more fun. I knew there had to be a soft side under Hayden's attitude. I just didn't expect my Samoyed dog to bring it out in him.

I take off my coat, hang it up, and fluff my hair as if that matters right now, then pull out some blankets as I get the fire going. I'm not sure what to do with Hayden right now. I know I want to know what he's proud of when it comes to his life, but should I make some alcoholic hot chocolate or pull some food out? We didn't eat dinner.

"Do you have a way to wipe his feet?" Hayden asks, making me jump.

"Uh, the towel with the dogs on it," I answer.

He takes care of Teddy's feet, talking to him the whole

time, so Teddy's excited and enjoying every second of it. After, Teddy does a freedom run and then brings Hayden a toy. Before I can warn him that fetch is a non-stop game, Hayden tosses the toy.

"Are you hungry?" I ask.

"I could eat," he answers.

I end up making us a frozen lasagna, but Hayden stays close. "Did you design all this?"

"Yup," I agree. "We're not in public. What are you most proud of?"

He sighs. "I'm charging you for this information, Molly."

I turn around, facing him as he boxes me in against the oven. I stare up at him and he leans down towards me, cupping my chin. I suck in a breath. "What's the cost?"

"You're not that dense," he purrs. "How badly do you want to know?"

He's built it up so much, I can't imagine not knowing. I hesitate which gives Hayden time to push the sleeves of his turtle neck up to his elbow. Black looks so good on him. I have a feeling that he'd look even better shirtless.

I take an unsteady breath. I only hated him for twenty-four hours, if that. What's wrong with me? Are my teenage fantasies that strong? I swallow. "I want to know."

He cocks his head to the side. "You're acting like kissing me is terrible."

"I wouldn't know, since I never-"

Hayden rolls his eyes and presses his lips to mine. He cups the nape of my neck, drawing me closer as his lips part mine. I put my hands on his chest, feeling how much muscle he has under his shirt. His tongue strokes between my lips, making my lips tingle before he licks deeper, teasing my tongue with his the same way he teased my finger earlier.

No one oversold his kissing ability, that's for damn sure. He presses me back against the stove, his body rubbing against mine as he renews the kiss, changing the angle so he can kiss me deeper. My stomach feels like it's melting as he sucks my tongue before nipping my bottom lip. I tighten my hold on his shirt and lean into the kiss, giving up on resisting Hayden.

I've wondered 'what if' for years, wanted to know how he'd kiss, how he'd feel for a decade? One of my hands slides up to his shoulder, and he lets out a throaty groan before kissing me faster, deeper. Everything is more until I can't remember why we started kissing and I don't care as long as he doesn't stop.

My whole body floods with heat until I want to rip off my clothes so we can keep making out. Hayden's hand tightens on the back of my neck as his other hand slides down my lower back to grab my ass, grinding me against his hardening cock.

I gasp, trying to save an ounce of sanity, but he works his tongue deeper into my mouth. The crisp scent of his cologne fills my nose as he draws me tighter against his hard, big body. With one more bite to my bottom lip, he releases me.

"Oh," I breathe, touching my bottom lip as I stare up at him.

He grins and kisses the corner of my mouth. "That earns you a lot of secrets, Molly."

"Like ..." I whisper, not trusting my voice.

"I'm the president of the Bull Sharks—a Motorcycle Club in Miami. That's what I'm proud of," he breathes.

FIVE

Hayden

I SHOULDN'T HAVE TOLD HER. I DON'T KNOW HOW SHE'LL react, but her brow furrows, and she stares up at me while still touching her bottom lip. "A motorcycle club?"

Right. "Motorcycle gang. We prefer club."

Her eyes widen. "Like all those shows and-"

"There's a lot less murder than in the shows," I promise, continuing to massage the back of her neck. "Don't get skittish on me now, Molly. I'm not going to hurt you."

"But that's what you're proud of?"

"Yes," I answer. "I had to work very hard to get there. It started as a hobby, but I *wanted* the title. C.E.O. is just how I make billions, so I can help more people. It's how people know me. It was supposed to be a made-up job that kept my bank account full, but people trust me with decision-making."

"Well, yeah," she answers.

"I worked from the bottom up in the club. I enjoy having an outlet for all my rebellious ways. Plus, we run a charity too. We escort kids who are providing testimony in court to make them feel safe. We're not *all* bad," I hum. "There are rules against involving innocent people."

"I see."

Forcing myself to take a step back is harder than I imagined. I've wanted Molly for years and now I give her a good reason to kick me out and distance herself. All because she didn't pump the breaks, all because she was so determined to get the answer she brought me to her place, kissed me, was so eager to know.

She blinks a few times and nods. "Sounds like you're meant to be in charge."

"In most areas, babe. Although, if you keep looking at me like that, I might be willing to tie my own wrists to see what you'll do with some power," I flirt, considering she's still wearing blush and her eyes are all dilated.

"Don't tease me like that. I feel like you're making fun of me," she huffs.

I arch an eyebrow. "Show me a scarf and I'll tie my wrists right here and now."

"You ... you're serious?"

"We have an hour to wait for the lasagna. We can be sweet and sit by the fire talking, or you and I can try something new," I croon. "I bet you haven't had total control over a single person in your life."

She takes an unsteady breath and points at me. "You're dangerous."

"In more ways than one," I tease with a wink.

"And you use flirting to avoid having a genuine conversation, so we're going to have a genuine conversation. I want to know everything about the M.C.. How you went from vandalism and breaking into places all the way to organized crime," she says.

"You don't want to know how I spend my billions?"

"I could look that up online. I *want* to know this," she argues.

Before I can try to seduce her again, she grabs my hand and drags me to the living room, in front of the fire. She pushes me down and Teddy brings a toy to me, his whole body wiggling in excitement as his tail wags. I toss it for him and Molly sits beside me, pulling a blanket around us. She points at me.

"I might just kiss you or ... pay you for the information. As long as you're honest."

"Molly, it makes me feel easy when you offer to kiss me or fuck me for information," I say.

"You were the one who set up the exchange in the first place?" She crosses her arms just under her breasts, pushing them up.

Yeah, I'm fucking easy where she's concerned. So I spill it all. How I joined the M.C. while in college after taking an invitation to a party I shouldn't have. From there, I got wrapped up in it, love the secrets, loved the wild side, the perks, all of it. I worked my way up, loved the previous president, and welcomed his teaching, his encouragement, and his lectures when I fell behind in school. He was more of a dad to me than my own.

Molly interrupts to ask questions or to clarify, staying focused on the story. When I finish, I shrug. "I won the vote for president, made the old man proud, and felt like I'd achieved something."

"So graduating college, working up a vast business, and becoming CEO is nothing to being president of that chapter?" she says, summarizing.

I nod once.

She considers that and nods. "It makes sense."

"Does it?"

"Well yeah. We're expected to graduate college and move up in whatever job we have. But becoming president of the chapter was more than a popularity contest. You had to work hard, fail a few times, then had to get better. Your dedication is impressive," she says, bumping me with her shoulder.

"And now the payment?" I ask.

She laughs. "You still have a one-track mind."

"Only where you're concerned," I mumble. "I never forgot you, Molly. All your attempts to reform me, the few times I caught you watching as I spray painted the side of a building, saying nothing until you were worried I'd get caught, the sad little face you'd make when some girl would fit herself to my side."

She snorts. "I'm sure you saw me as a little kid. I'm four years younger."

"The age difference kept me in check, but we're adults now," I say. "Four years is nothing."

Her eyes catch the firelight as she looks up at me, an innocent edge to the desire in her eyes. I stroke her cheek. "Do I still scare you?"

"No," she answers.

"Not even with all the tattoos?"

"They're pretty," she argues, stroking my exposed arm and raising goosebumps on my skin. "Just like your curly hair, the green flecks in your eyes, and ..."

I lean forward and kiss her. She kisses me back, with no hesitation, just her mouth on mine. She ends up in my lap, feeding me kiss after kiss. I pull at her dress while she tugs at my turtle neck. Her lips brush mine as she speaks. "I want to see all your tattoos, Hayden."

"And I thought you were innocent," I growl, helping her pull off my turtleneck.

She strokes over my chest, following swirls of color and thick lines of black, then sliding her fingers down to my abs. I'm painfully hard just from kissing her and feeling her fingers dance across my skin.

Molly's sapphire eyes meet mine as I stroke through her soft hair. "You're still too damn good for me."

"Never," she disagrees.

Just before she can kiss me again, the oven timer goes off. She stands up in front of me, and I kiss her thigh through her leggings. Her breath catches and she strokes through my hair.

"Eat the lasagna first."

"I'll let you get it out of the oven. After that, all bets are off," I growl.

She somehow ropes me into eating dinner instead of her. I try to cool my lust by burning the hell out of my mouth with the lasagna. It doesn't work when she moans around her fork. I think she's baiting me, seeing how long I can hold out.

After one piece of lasagna, I'm done.

"Did you get me a scarf?" I ask.

She looks at me, eyes dipping to my body before jumping back to my face.

"They're all in my bedroom," she whispers. "We ... we could go there."

"You're hesitant," I point out.

"Because you're leaving in less than two weeks," she says. "I don't just ..."

"I'm a billionaire, Molly. If you want me back here, I have a plane I can use."

Her eyes widen. She doesn't finish her lasagna. She just takes my plate, walks to the kitchen and puts the lasagna on the back burner of her oven. She looks up at me once she realizes I've followed her.

"Do you just want to fuck me? Is that what this is, Hayden? You didn't get to before and now you have a chance and want to capitalize on it?"

"Did I say that?"

"I have to bait you or bribe you or drink with you to get you to say anything real!" she exclaims. "I can't read your mind, so tell me."

"Molly," I sigh.

"This matters to me! I don't just sleep around. I get hit on plenty and I have a three-date rule at minimum and-"

"Ice skating." I hold up a finger before taking a step towards her. "Hot chocolate and walking through town," another finger goes up and I take another step forward.

"Playing with your dog and having dinner." that's three fingers up and I'm close enough that our bodies nearly touch. "I've spent more time with you than my family while here. If I just wanted to get laid, I'd use a damn hookup app."

"I didn't say you just wanted to get laid. I'm asking if you're going to leave the second after we finish. I'm asking if you're only doing all of this to get in my pants. I'm asking ..."

She trails off and looks away. She wants to know if I like her. If it's possible for me to like her—as she is—after two days. I like her *enough* that I don't want to think about leaving tonight. I'm not going to sneak out while she's showering or once she falls asleep. I want to make her breakfast in the morning.

Hell, I could enjoy this trip with her.

"I'm staying for breakfast, if you let me," I say.

She swallows, studying my eyes. "You make me stupid."

"Ditto, babe," I reply. "I've never offered to tie my own wrists for someone. Even as a joke."

She shakes her head. "You're intense."

"Very, and I'm happy to show you where I want to focus my intensity," I growl.

She closes the space between us. "I've done stupider things than this, though."

"I'll listen to every single story you want to tell me," I say, rubbing her lower back. "In the morning, over French toast and eggs."

She lets out a soft little moan and I don't care if it's because of me or the promise of a big breakfast. I can't spend another moment waiting to taste her again. I press my mouth to hers in a punishing kiss, kissing her deeper, trying to give her a bit of everything she needs. The ball is in her court, but I'm not nice enough to stay back when I want her, when I'm craving her, when every minute with her makes her even better.

Molly melts against me, pulling me closer. The second I

get to taste the little whimper that leaves her lips, I draw back. "Yes or no, babe?"

"Yes," she murmurs, "but you are going to show me whatever you have in mind with your wrists first."

I grin and she leads me upstairs, pulling a doggy gate out to give us some privacy from Teddy. She hands me a black scarf and I use a quick trick I've learned, slide my hands into the two loops I've created, then lift the long end of the scarf to my mouth to tighten it around my wrists. Molly stares at my hands, grabs my arms, then pulls me close.

She kisses me again, setting the pace before she pushes me back onto her bed. She takes an uneven breath, then peels off her leggings before gripping the hem of her dress. I groan. "Please, don't stop."

She takes off her dress, revealing mismatched underwear that looks so damn sexy on her. I don't think I want to see her in anything else ... unless she's naked.

Molly lies next to me, takes my tied wrists and holds them over my head. "Are you sure about giving me control?"

As I consider it, she kisses my chest, her tongue tracing some of my ink. I groan. "I've never been more sure of a damn thing."

SIX

Molly

I keep kissing down Hayden's body. In all honesty, I do not know what to do with this kind of power, but feeling his stomach tighten as I touch and kiss him feels amazing. Knowing he's enjoying it—this man that I thought was out of my league for so long—all because of what I'm doing-feels like a victory.

I tug on his belt, and he lifts his hips. "Fuck, you're driving me insane, Molly."

Goosebumps rise on my skin as I drag his zipper down. "Why do I think you're going to end up getting your wrists free?"

"Because you're smart as hell," he murmurs. "I'll try to be patient."

"Keep your hands up there or I won't finish stripping," I say, hoping I sound more resolute than I feel.

He gives me a naughty smile. "Tommy was right. You're demanding."

I bite his hip and he hisses, lifting his hips again so I can drag his jeans and boxers down in one go. As I jerk his clothes down to his ankles, I step back. He kicks off his clothes so he's lying there naked. Muscular, tattooed, Hayden Grant is stretched out over my bed, wrists bound, staring at me as his cock taps his belly.

He's long, pretty thick, and ... my mouth waters just looking at him. I'm no virgin, but I've never appreciated the way a naked man looks before. Hayden's gorgeous. If I could draw or paint or sculpt, I'd want him to be my model. His intense eyes darken as some of his dark hair falls in his face.

"You're too far away, babe. I'm losing patience," he growls.

I climb back onto the bed and run my fingers over the vein in his cock. He takes a sharp breath in response. I let my tongue follow the same path, and he moans. "Blow me."

"I'm the one in charge," I argue, before running my lips along the other side of his dick. "Patience is rewarded."

"And I love your rewards," he hums, his head falling back as I lick over the tip. "So fucking much."

I tease him with soft licks and *almost* take him in my mouth until he's frustrated, his face red, jaw clenched, and eyes full of threats. After giving him a smile, I grab my hair in one hand, spread my lips around his cock, then sink down on him. I don't stop until he's choking me, filling my mouth and throat, I moan with him.

"So damn good," he rasps, flexing his hips to drive himself deeper into my mouth.

I blow him, taking my time so I can suck, lick, tease. He groans and grips the pillow behind his head to keep his hands in place, but his biceps flex as his abs ripple, and I'm torn between focusing on his cock and licking every inch of him.

"I want you naked," he growls.

I take him deeper until he stops trying to make me obey. I like feeling him move across my tongue, feeling the slight pulse in his cock, like he's already going to blow. After he groans again, I pop off him.

Standing up, I take off my bra, then wiggle out of my panties. I almost wish I would have kept going to that workout class with Tamsin to lose just five more pounds, but Hayden's watching me like I'm a goddess he's ready to worship.

Who needs to work out if a few extra pounds gets me this much attention? I step on my bed, straddling him, then grab the scarf around his wrists, jerking him forward. "You said you were hungry, right?"

"Fucking starving," he agrees.

He doesn't need any other instruction. Hayden licks over my slit, the tip of his tongue brushing my clit. He groans and laps at my pussy. I've been wet since the first kiss he gave me in the kitchen, aching for his touch, his attention, everything, but none of it prepared me for his mouth. Every suck and flick of his tongue drives me insane until my thighs are shaking and I have to brace myself on the wall behind him just to stay standing.

"So delicious," he pants before returning to his feast.

He grabs my ass and I see that the scarf is lying on the bed. I can't even complain. All I can do is moan as he guides me over his tongue. With one hard jerk on my hips, he pulls me down on his face.

I gasp and try to push myself up, worried I'm going to crush him, but he doesn't let me move, his grip iron as he continues eating me out until my eyes roll back and I moan his name. The first orgasm is easy. The second one, with his fingers teasing my pussy, rubbing gently before thrusting in deep-is overwhelming, consuming—heat racing through my body until I'm convinced it's summer.

My vision darkens, and I surrender to the ecstasy of Hayden's mouth and fingers.

When I come to, I'm on my back, comfortable on my bed. My thighs tremble, and I stare up at Hayden. "You took off your cuffs."

"I wanted you to ride my face, babe. I couldn't resist," he says before wiping his bottom lip with his thumb. He sucks his finger, then gives me a wolfish smile. "And I want more."

Hayden grabs my ankles and spreads my legs. He slides between my thighs and kisses across my chest, cupping my breasts in his hands. He sucks my nipple between his moist lips and grazes me with his teeth.

"Hayden," I pant.

He switches to the other, lavishing me with attention until his name is the only word on my lips. Hayden shows me the pitiful restraints that lasted less than twenty minutes. He grabs my wrists, puts them on, and tightens them with his teeth. I gasp.

"But-"

He pushes my restraints above my head and kisses me, his tongue teasing mine as he grinds against me, his cock rubbing against my clit, teasing me every time he moves. He draws back and grins. "But what?"

"I want to touch you," I complain.

"Then escape the restraints. It's not too hard," he hums.

I tug at them, lifting my hands, but Hayden licks over my nipple again as the head of his cock presses against my entrance. I whimper and wiggle against him, wanting a lot more. He keeps kissing my chest, my shoulders, and my neck, all while easing deeper inside me.

"Hayden," I moan. "Stop teasing."

He grins and thrusts all the way inside me, making us both moan. When I try to touch him, he grabs my wrists and holds them above my head. "It's my turn to be in charge, baby."

"Please," I whimper.

He slams into me, making my back arch as he fills me. He feels better than I hoped. Hayden sets a pace that has me shaking, moaning, and teetering on cloud nine. His lips brush my ear. "Once won't be enough with you, Molly. I want to fuck you against every window in this house, in every room, in every position we can think of."

"Yes," I whine, lifting my hips and trying to hold his hand.

He slides his fingers between mine and grabs my ass, pulling me against him so I can meet every thrust. "Please!"

"Every day I'm here, I'm yours," he promises against my mouth before kissing me senseless.

In another second, I'm on top of him, riding him. I roll my hips against him, loving his panting breaths, the way he can't seem to stop kissing me, touching me. He bites my ear. "Nothing's enough with you. I want more."

"Show me," I order him, slipping one wrist free of the restraints to wrap my arm around his neck.

He reaches between us to rub my clit as he continues bouncing me on him. My head falls back and I dig my nails into his shoulder, needing something to hold on to as I increase the pace.

"Molly, fuck!" he yells, slamming me back down on the bed.

He pulls out, earning a whine from me that makes him chuckle. "I'm not done. We have all night."

Hayden flips me over, jerks my hips back, and fills me again. He fucks me harder, getting so much deeper at this angle even as my knees slip on the sheets. He bends over me, kissing and nipping the back of my shoulder. My fingers knot in the sheets as he palms my breast, pinching my nipple, teasing me until I can't hold out anymore.

"Hayden!"

"Come for me. Right now. It won't be the last time," he swears in that low gravelly voice.

His fingers brush my clit and it's enough to make me come. I press my face to my pillow as I yell his name. He groans and jerks me back, pounding into me, taking my orgasm higher and higher until I'm dizzy.

Just before I can come down from the high, Hayden jerks out of me and comes on my ass. He swats my butt and releases a low groan as he rubs against my ass. We collapse together in bed, too hot for even a blanket.

Hayden turns my chin and feeds me soft kisses, each deeper than the last until I find myself on top of him again. I draw back, sucking my bottom lip. "That was ..."

"So damn good," he sighs.

I nod in agreement. I'm still worried he's going to leave despite all his promises. Words are words. They're easy to ignore. It's why I don't want to jump in the shower, let my eyes close too long, or get too comfortable.

Hayden rubs my back. "You didn't finish your food."

"Your fault."

He gives me a wide smile. "I'm not sorry for that. Why don't you get a shower and I'll bring your food up."

Again, I hesitate. He shrugs and cuddles me, continuing to kiss me, touch me, looking at peace. I just had sex with a C.E.O., the president of a motorcycle gang, the man I thought I'd never see again.

"I should clean up," I say after a while, my voice sticking in my throat.

"Your house—your rules," he answers.

I head to the bathroom after wrapping up in a sheet, glancing back at him once. His eyes rake over me and he licks his bottom lip. Maybe I should be more worried about my shower being interrupted than him leaving.

Not that it stops me from rushing. Not that me rushing would stop him from leaving if he was determined. When I walk back into my room, looking for pajamas, I hear Hayden downstairs.

"I know, Teddy. It's not fair you don't get lasagna, but I kind of want your human to like me," he says. "Which means I can't feed you people food."

I pull on a tank top and some silk pajama pants while smiling.

"Don't give me the puppy-dog eyes. They'll work for Molly, not you ..." he trails off and groans. "Where are your fucking treats?"

I head downstairs and find him in jeans, telling Teddy to sit before tossing him a treat. He motions to the microwave when he sees me. "I'm not giving you cold food."

"Thank you," I whisper.

"Do you have the ingredients we need for breakfast?" he peeks into the fridge as Teddy noses my thigh. I pet my dog while watching Hayden make note of the food in my fridge.

Maybe, just maybe, Hayden could be a dream come true.

SEVEN

Hayden

When I wake up in the morning, Molly is still asleep, each even breath blowing across my arm. I forgot I'd let her use my arm as a pillow. I ease away from her, kissing the back of her shoulder and bunching the blanket around her.

I jerk on my clothes head downstairs and take Teddy out, then get started on breakfast until my phone rings. I look at it. The vice president of our chapter is asking if we're doing the toy drive this year. I type back an affirmative and get a thumbs up.

My assistant hasn't texted or emailed me from my company job, but I send her a reminder to send out the donations to the local orphanages and to a few charities that give low-income families great Christmases.

"Deck the halls," I grunt.

"I know that wasn't part of a Christmas song, Grinch," Molly says.

I jump and turn, seeing her in a long-sleeved crop top and high-waisted pants. She looks delectable. We're getting back in bed after breakfast. I lean back on the counter and grin. "I don't remember giving you permission to leave the bed."

"I don't remember needing it in my house," she says before tapping my chest.

I steal a long kiss, devouring her. I don't know how it's possible for anyone to keep their hands off her. She looks so damn good, especially softened by sleep, her blonde hair a mess.

"Mmm," she hums as she draws back. "Teddy, let's go-"

"I already took him out," I grumble.

She gapes at me, then a glint sparkles in her eyes, the same sparkle she had when she walked to the shower last night. I sigh. "Go ahead and ask."

She shakes her head, then banishes the look before giving me a half-hearted smile. "I'm going to think you're with me for my dog, Hayden."

We eat breakfast, but I still see a question in Molly's gaze. I set my coffee down. "Still overthinking the Christmas thing?"

"You told me bah humbug when I wished you a Merry Christmas, then you say "deck the halls" this morning. It's just leaving me kind of confused about why you hate Christmas so much. What made you a grinch?"

I hesitate before answering. There's an appeal to one night stands or having a fling with a woman who didn't know me. I enjoy being with Molly, *wanted* to be right here, but didn't want this conversation. I clear my throat. "It wasn't just one thing. Nothing traumatic."

Molly pets her dog, who keeps trying to get into her lap to steal bacon, and I continue. "When I was little, it was great. I loved Christmas. Everyone got along–better than ever before. My father would smile and play with us, my mom would bake in the kitchen and the entire house felt warm. All the decorations at school, the snow days made great with friends, the decorations, even Santa. I loved it all."

"So what changed?"

"Well, fewer and fewer relatives would come over as the years went on. I was told I needed to 'man up' and do more–

chopping wood, ignoring the movies to clean up and prepare for our guests. My dad started asking what I was going to do with my life; when I was going to grow up. Over the years it became a time of year where every single thing I did wrong over the past year came back to bite me in conversations with relatives. The presents became less magical, the songs seemed to rub in my face how cold my family was, and with the pressure to buy presents, be perfect, do everything ..."

I'm not sure I'm saying it right at all. But Molly leans forward, not eating, just watching me. I cleared my throat. "It became all about appearances and money spent and accomplishments and who was the most successful. My parents weren't as shiny and bright as they used to be, and everyone talking about the 'spirit' of Christmas, all the new movies about love and romance, the people excited ... I don't know if it was jealousy or me becoming more cynical, or the inability to escape everyone else being happy, but ... I hate it."

She nods a few times. "I guess I can understand that."

"How? You were a golden child. I knew if I was like you in high school, if I was half as good as you, that things would be different," I mumble.

Molly gets up and sits on my lap. I wrap my arms around her. "How about you, hmm? Why do you love Christmas?"

"I get to be around the people I love—the people I choose—and celebrate everything. Last year, we celebrated Tamsin breaking up with a not great guy. Charlotte celebrated moving here after being away at college. Angela celebrated getting through the hardest year yet with the bakery. But we all survived it and we had a new year to look forward to soon. We got each other hand made presents, we got to celebrate and spend time together."

"That sounds nice," I admit.

"You don't have to celebrate with your family, Hayden," Molly whispers. "You're an adult, you get to choose."

My first instinct is to tell her she's wrong, that she doesn't understand, but I don't say it right away. Molly kisses my neck. "You can visit them, then come to the bakery, or here. Winter might not be a choice, but Christmas is."

"Be careful, being so sweet. I might have to fuck it out of you," I wink and chuckle as I tickle her.

She feeds me bacon. "Eat first. We already went two rounds last night, and shockingly, I don't have all day to be in bed with you, Hayden."

"Is that a fact?"

"I have a festival to finish planning, some crafting to do, vendors to confirm, I have to check the tree, and I have at least six emails from potential clients to go through," she says. "Not as easy as when we were in high school."

"Am I being rushed out of your house?" I question.

"Maybe you are, unless you want to help me with errands," she says while offering me a bite of French toast.

Since my options are going to my hotel and thinking about Molly, going to my parents and overthinking what she just said, or going with her, the answer seems pretty clear. I ask if Teddy can go too, and she agrees.

When we get to town, I get to see how much Molly has changed. She wears the same warm smile but isn't afraid to be straightforward. She doesn't hesitate to say 'no' when something isn't right.

She's ambitious, sure of herself, and non-stop. Even then, when someone throws me a glance and mutters about 'trouble' being back in town, Molly just takes my hand and introduces me, like I've never met these shop owners before—the same shop owners I stole from and vandalized.

It feels like ten years too late to give an apology.

Molly warms them up anyway, then leads me to 'Heavenly Sweets', the best bakery in town. She squeezes my arm. "How are you not freezing?"

"You're keeping me nice and warm, Molly," I growl.

I'm not about PDA or letting my soft side show where

others can see. I clear my throat. "So, you've bullied three shop owners. Are you going to ask Angela to make things too?"

She scoffs. "I didn't *bully* anyone. I convinced them. Firmly, but sweetly."

"Show me some of that firm and sweet," I growl in her ear.

She blushes and I want to take all the credit for it, but with the bitter cold and the wind, I'm not sure. Teddy tugs on his leash, eager to get to the store. Molly takes my hand and laces our fingers together. "Angela spoils him with treats."

"Ah, I have competition for his affection," I mumble.

Molly bumps my hip. "You listen here. If I'm not Teddy's favorite, there's a problem."

Molly drags me into the bakery, talks with Angela who keeps looking at me like she had a camera in the bedroom while I was fucking her best friend. I clear my throat. "Coffee?"

She gets us coffee and Molly swats me. "That's all you can say?"

"She's looking at me like she's undressing me with her eyes, babe," I murmur.

Molly looks me over and cocks her head to the side. "You are wearing the same clothes as yesterday and you smell like cookies, Hayden."

"Your body wash," I say.

She bites her lip and whispers in my ear. "I like how it smells on you. Maybe I should ask Angela to watch Teddy so you can show me your hotel room."

"Are you hitting on me?" I demand, as if it's scandalous.

"I'm about five seconds away from grabbing your ass, sending Angela on an errand and turning that open sign to 'closed'," she whispers, her voice all breathy and warm. "I don't get you for long, so I have to make the most of it."

"Not innocent or sunny today, are you?" I ask, my hand

sliding into her back pocket. She jumps as I squeeze her ass. "I think I'll have to punish you for being so naughty."

"And how are you going to do that, grinch? Take away all my toys?" she asks.

"Oh, if you have toys and you're holding out on me ..."

"Don't you two look cute," Angela interrupts us.

Molly's face flares red and this time I know it's thanks to me. She clears her throat as I take my coffee and pay Angela. Molly forces herself to speak even if her voice is a little higher pitched than normal. "Would you mind watching Teddy tonight?"

"Well, if it's for what I think it's for, then I'm happy to," Angela giggles before reaching around to take Teddy's leash from me.

He jumps up on her, his big paws on her upper arms. She ruffles his ears. "We're going to have lots of fun. We can go sledding, you'll get tons of treats, I'll even let you on my bed."

"I'll let you on my bed too," I purr in Molly's ears, making her cheeks go red. "Come on. Errands are done."

"But I should check on-"

"Give me your to-do list and live. Go on. Enjoy the holidays instead of planning them," Angela orders her.

Molly looks at me and bites her bottom lip. "I'm willing to take a risk with you, Hayden."

With that, I take her hand and lead her to her car. The second she gets in the driver's side, I pull her towards me and kiss her hard, hungry. I don't care who sees us making out in a car. It's not sweet, so it's fine.

She moans and leans into the kiss, running her fingers over my jaw until she pulls me closer. I don't know if we're even going to make it to the hotel at this rate. It's only been a few hours since we left her place and I'm so ready to have her again, to make every other person at the hotel hate us, check out, and leave the whole place to us and us alone as long as I'm here.

"Molly, you keep this up ..."

"Car sex isn't possible. Too many layers," she rasps against my mouth.

"Yup, you need to speed," I decide.

She laughs, but drives at a normal pace, driving me wild. I rub her thigh as I give her instructions to get to the hotel. Once we park, I unbuckle her, drag her across the seat so she's straddling me and kiss her.

"I think you should learn to celebrate the holidays my way."

"I will," she breathes against my mouth. "If you come with me to the tree lighting in two days."

I pause. I don't want to go. My parents will be there, plenty of people will be there, and I'd rather have a reason to avoid it, but seeing the excitement in Molly's eyes, along with my dick demanding satisfaction, makes the decision for me. "Deal."

EIGHT

Molly

We make it to his huge hotel room. There's zero romance put into it. Hayden has me against the wall, kissing me his lips slide over mine as he peels off my coat, then my sweater. My shirt sticks to it, but he just rips that off, too.

"I need you *now*," he growls.

"Make me warm," I beg.

"You won't feel a trace of the cold," Hayden says, lighting the ornate fireplace in his room. The fire roars and he picks me up and carries me to his bed. He comes down on top of me, kissing me like he needs me to survive. "You'll only feel me, baby."

"Faster," I beg, desperate for him to take his clothes off.

I peel his shirt off him and kiss his muscular chest, up his neck, and plan to bite his ear when he grabs my face between his hands to kiss me again. I groan as his tongue meets mine. Hayden somehow—like some kind of magician—gets us both naked while keeping me distracted with kisses that have me wet and eager for more.

"Fuck me," I whisper against his mouth.

"Still full of demands. I might just have to tie you up," he teases while kissing across my breasts.

"If it gets you to fuck me, then do it!"

He laughs, but obeys, slamming into me, so my back arches. He groans. "So fucking wet for me, baby," he growls in my ear.

"Just you," I whine.

"That's right, because you're mine, entirely and totally mine," he says before biting the top of my breast.

Hayden fucks like it's a job he loves to do. He touches me, makes my pleasure his priority, but then tosses restraint to the side and takes me the way he needs to come. Which is how we spend the afternoon and night.

We have sex in his bed, against a window, in front of his fireplace–as he first promised–and anywhere else he can think of until even his lips on my skin is too much for my oversensitive body.

"You look good freshly fucked," Hayden croons while putting my wine glass to my lips.

"And you ... you should not be able to keep going like an energizer bunny!" I exclaim.

He laughs and kisses up my neck. I rub his hand after a bit and see that he put on the Grinch. I swat at him, but he chuckles. "You keep calling me a grinch, so we'll watch it as long as it's fun."

"Yeah, when does it stop being fun?" I ask.

"Right after he saves the little girl, then they go to the heart growing, and that's just not for me," he snorts.

I try to wrestle some Christmas spirit into him until there's a knock on the door and Hayden reappears with food. I blink at him. "There's no room service here."

"I know. I had my driver go pick it up. Money moves mountains, babe."

Rolling my eyes feels like a good way to respond, but I can't complain when the food is so delicious. I'd be happy to be with Hayden, like this - this warm, cuddly, half dressed version I get when we're alone - forever.

It's been two days, and already he's making me think of absolute nonsense.

But on day three, my heart squeezes when he asks about old shops in town. On day four, when he criticizes the Christmas tree only to wink at me, I feel my whole body heat. As he takes my hand and reluctantly goes to the tree lighting festival with me, I can't shake off the new excitement I feel. Daily sex is great, especially with Hayden, but the fact that he's *trying* to let the Christmas spirit live means so much more.

He pauses when he sees the crowds, though. "Molly ..."

"What's wrong?"

"I've been avoiding my parents since our talk and ... I know they're going to be here with my sister. If they see me with you..."

He mentioned his parents wouldn't have been so hard on him if he was like me, so why would them seeing us together be a bad thing? I swallow and meet his eyes. "Would it be that terrible? I thought ..."

"This isn't just sex," he says, something that's come up more than I want to admit. "You know that. I'm going to fly you down to Miami under the guise of repurposing my building to hold you hostage for a month. Then I'm going to find a way to come right back here ... but if my parents see us together, they're going to get the idea that I'm staying."

"Is staying that terrible? I mean, if we're going to be in a relationship, then we'll move in together. Why would the idea be so terrible?"

His face goes white and pushes his lips into a firm line. He doesn't say anything, just lets Teddy drag him forward. As I try to show Hayden great things—the hot cocoa stand, the marshmallow Santas and snowmen, the children's choir— he just keeps looking around like a lost meerkat.

"Ooh, are things going well?" Tamsin asks, making me jump.

"Where did you come from?" I demand.

"I'm on chili duty. Apparently, people love it in the winter. Who knew?" she asks with a shrug. "Angela told me you and Hayden have been a packaged deal, so it looks like you got your wish."

"Something like that."

"You don't sound happy. Is the sex good at least?" she asks.

"The sex is great, it's ... nothing."

"Yeah, you saying 'nothing' leads to fights," she counters. "What is it? I take kick boxing, if he's hurt you-"

"Hey, Tam-Tam," Hayden greets her before wrapping his arm around my waist. It's the most he's touched me in public since he got here.

"No. It's Tam*sin*. I know if you try hard you can say it," she says sarcastically. "In fact, I swear you've said it before."

He rolls his eyes. "Are you freezing yet?"

"Nope, the chili's keeping me warm. Have some," she orders him, putting a mug of chili in both our hands. She sticks plastic spoons in both and waves us on.

"She's fun," Hayden says with an approving smile. "I like her bite. She'd whip business men into shape."

"Are you okay?" I ask.

"Yeah, babe. I'm okay," he assures me. "Why wouldn't I be?"

"Because this is the first time you've touched me since we got here. I know you're not big on PDA, but considering you got angry that Tommy hugged me and whispered in my ear the other night at the bar-"

"Because Tommy's had a longstanding crush on you, just like me," he huffs.

"Hayden, please, be honest with me," I whisper before shoving chili into my mouth. It's way too hot. I fan my mouth.

Hayden turns my chin up, kisses me slowly, then gives me a soft peck before releasing me. The burn of the spicy chili subsides and Hayden pulls away. "I'm not ashamed to be seen with you, Molls. I've been by your side for three days now ... well, this makes four, I guess."

"I'm afraid that the second your parents come, you're going to run away, with or without my dog," I grumble.

He clears his throat and looks away. I grab his arm and pull him over to the side. "Hayden, seriously. You said you're not in this for sex, so why can't they see us together? Just tell them you're not staying, that we're going to do long distance ... if we're even in relationship territory and not just.."

"If you say just 'having sex' again," he warns me, that dark lusty look in his eyes. He likes to punish me a specific way—by putting me over his knee and spanking me until I beg him to do more than edge me with his fingers and swat my ass—and I already see that delicious threat in his eyes.

"I'm not saying that. If we're more than friends with benefits."

"We're dating. We're exclusive. You're mine and I'll start saying it when I'm not inside you if that makes it clear," he says sharply, with an arch of his eyebrow.

I stare at him, not sure how to respond. He takes a slow breath.

"Why are you so angry about this?" I ask.

His eyes focus on me as his hands curl into fists and he stands taller. "I don't want my parents getting disappointed with me *again*, Molly. They'll see us together, assume we're an item, assume I'm going to stay, move the business here and maybe move back in! I already have to deal with fucking Christmas here. I don't want to deal with that too!"

And there's the Hayden Grant I remember. The one who would lash out when things didn't go his way, the one who has a temper shorter than anyone I've ever met before. I can't curb it with sex. I can't curb it by showing him how great things can be. He's still bitter, still holding his past against Christmas and his family.

"Don't make that face," he whispers as he stops huffing and puffing and meets my eyes.

"Go have a smoke and cool down," I order.

"Baby-"

"You don't get to yell at me, so go smoke, calm down, and find me when you can have an adult conversation," I keep my voice even.

Hayden hands me the leash and walks off, already pulling out his cigarettes. I take a few deep breaths, then get closer to the tree. Hayden and I can't work out, can we? No matter how good the sex is, no matter how wonderful he can be, he still has a stick up his ass where his family is concerned. I don't think it's Christmas. I don't think it's Mistletoe Meadows, I think it's them ... them and their shared past.

He can't escape it, he can't run away from it even in Miami, and I don't just want to be with Hayden when everything is going well with him. That's not how relationships work. We won't always be on vacation, he won't always have this freedom, and if this hard-headed, has-to-be-in control, gets-to-dictate-everything side of him is the one he shows, that's not the person I want to be with.

I stand in front of the tree and Charlotte bounces to my side as I notice some people looking at me with a mix of confusion and concern. Charlotte giggles. "You know, everyone's talking about you and Hayden Grant getting together. Is it love? Is it Lust?"

"Lottie," I start.

"Come on, I won't tell anyone. I just want to know," she insists.

"Charlotte it's not the-"

"It's a hell of a lot more than lust," Hayden says. I stare at him in surprise as he wraps his arms around me. "That's what you and everyone should know. Molly is mine. My girlfriend."

The word bounces in my head like a ping bong ball until it makes sense. Girlfriend? He's committing to me. Charlotte bounces. "I knew it! And if you have her and Teddy's approval, you must be a lot better than people think."

Charlotte hurries off to Angela and I'm sure even his parents will know in the next hour. I turn in Hayden's arms. "You were supposed to be smoking."

"Yeah, I got through half a cigarette before realizing that if I let you walk away, I might not get another chance. I will not leave you again, Molly. I can't do another ten years of 'what if's. I don't think I'd last even a week this time. I'm not taking the chance that someone else is going to see how amazing, sweet, sexy, controlling, organized ... maddening and wonderful you are," he says.

My heart lodges in my throat just as snow collects in his dark hair.

Four days and I'm sure I'm in love with this man. Maybe I can love the bad parts too.

NINE

Hayden

____

MOLLY CONTINUES TO STARE AT ME, HER PRETTY LIPS PARTED.
Kissing her is probably the wrong move after a half fight. I did
all the yelling, and she did the calming. That's not how it's
supposed to go. We both yell, get out everything we need to
say, then move on.

"You know we have to talk about things, right? Real
things, like why you're so angry at your family," she breathes.

"That sounds like hell," I mumble.

"You only stop being angry if you work through the anger,
Hayden. I can't be with someone who snaps like that. I won't
... even if I want to," she says, her nose going red.

I lift her chin, wanting her to focus on me. "I'll talk to you
about it, but we need time before we dive into all that. I'll
make sure we have it. I'll fly to you every weekend, fly you to
me when you have time. You don't have to move."

"And in the future if or when-" she starts.

"No. We're not going that far yet. Let's see how things go.
If we get all pissy over things that might not happen, we're
dooming ourselves before we can stop it. So let's ... just see
where this takes us. We haven't even been dating a week," I
counter.

"Your parents are here."

"And until I meet yours, there's no reason for us to talk to mine. Not *yet*," I emphasize. "We will. And I won't run from it, Molly. I won't run from you or Teddy. I'm just starting to believe I'm relationship material and Christmas might not be overrated. Can that be enough for right now?"

She blinks at me, computing before nodding. "You have catching up to do. I can understand that."

"You'll have to catch up to my lifestyle in Miami, so I think it's fair," I tease.

She bites her bottom lip. "Is it too much to ask you to hold my hand and kiss me when the Christmas tree lights up?"

"Considering the whole town knows that you're turning me from delinquent to civilized man, I think that's perfect to ask." I chuckle.

She swats me. "You're not that civilized, Mr. billionaire."

As we wait for the tree to turn on, Molly tells me everything that went into this moment, how much planning had to be done, the generator to light the tree since she was nervous about knocking the whole town's power out, like someone did four years ago, all the favors she now owes people.

When they start the countdown, I pull Molly close. "Who do you want to kiss more: me or Teddy?"

"It's close," she says with a teasing smile. "I think you win by a hair."

"I'll be here for the New Year," I promise as I lean in and kiss her, not waiting for some light to tell me to do it.

She melts against me, kissing me back, matching every stroke of my tongue and devouring me until the music plays. I pull back and let her watch as the tree lights up and moves in sync with the music. When she shivers, I pull her into my arms and hold her against my chest.

"It's beautiful," she mumbles.

I look down at her, watching the lights play across her face, dance in her amazed eyes. Snowflakes catch on her lashes as her face goes pink. She's a better view. I can't imagine picking the sunset or the ocean over her. I can't imagine missing anything more than I'll miss her when I go back to Miami.

If I wasn't a wealthy man, it would be impossible to leave without her. Angela brings us hot chocolates and teases us about me losing cool points by being cute. I just roll my eyes and tighten my arm around Molly.

"I see your mom," Molly informs me.

I follow her gaze and see my family there. My mom watches me with confusion and traces of betrayal, but I don't care. I'm going to stay right where I am, wrapped around Molly. It's half because Teddy's leash is wrapped around us, but also because I don't want Molly looking at me like I'm breaking her heart again.

So I keep her close all night, artfully avoid my family until Molly treats it like a game.

After the festival, we get back to her place and I help her take off her boots, then go for the rest of her clothes. She squeals and bats at me. "I'm freezing, Hayden!"

"All the more reason to get naked. It's the best way to share body heat," I wink.

She swats at me until I strip.

After a round of astoundingly satisfying sex, we curl up in her heaviest blanket in front of the fireplace. Molly looks at me and nuzzles my neck. "I can't believe you're leaving in four days."

"I know," I admit. "I'm thinking about taking care of my business over a computer so I can stay until New Year's Eve."

She perks. "Really?"

"Really. Though, I'm not loving staying at the hotel," I hint. "It's not the price, but it feels cramped."

She rolls her eyes. "Just ask."

"I don't know what you mean."

"Liar," she scolds. "Don't make me bribe you."

I look over her naked body, her perfect breasts, marked by

my teeth and mouth, the cute little roll in her belly, her thick thighs, and-

"You stop looking at me like that," she orders, wrapping an arm around her belly.

I push her down and pull her arm off her belly. "You don't get to deny me a gorgeous view."

"That's-"

"Let me stay with you, Molly. I'll wake you up every morning in a way I know you'll like," I promise.

She pretends to think about it. "I don't know."

"Then you get a demonstration," I decide, burying my face between her legs and devouring her pussy.

I love how she moans and bucks against me. I love how she chants my name, squirms, rubs herself against my tongue. No matter how much she says it's too much, I keep going until she comes for me, letting out a soft yell.

I wink at her as I lick my lips. "Does that mean I can stay?"

"Every ... single ... morning," she insists, kissing me with each word.

Moving in the next day is fun and easy. Molly has to take care of things for Christmas. She reads out a list that makes almost no sense to me, kisses my cheek, and hurries off. I take care of some work, using her home computer, then look at her sketches, her pieces of work.

Seeing how she brings her visions to life time and time again has me falling for her all over again.

Things go well until Christmas Eve. I get back to her place after taking Teddy in to town to get her a present and surprise her with cookies, but find Molly setting up her own tree, singing to herself.

She only has upbeat, fun songs playing and, for a minute, after watching her dance around the tree while decorating, I almost think I could love Christmas as much as I love her. The thought reverberates through me. I love her. As stupid as it is after so few days, it's true. I've never felt like this. Guys like me don't get to have all this.

Molly notices me and stops dancing. Her cheeks go pink, then a shade of red. "I thought you'd be longer. I thought you were with your parents or-"

I cross the space between us and kiss her like I'm starving for her. Enjoying the taste of her moans, I like kissing *her*. She feels so right against me. I groan and pull her tighter. Something smacks my shoulder, and I draw back to see an ornament.

"Are you still working on the tree?" I ask.

"Yes." She narrows her eyes at me. "Do not knock it over like an angry cat."

"I want to help. You make it look like fun," I say.

She beams brighter than any star or tree. We finish the tree together and I show her the cookies. She smiles, insists on making cider for us, then we sit down with the light of the tree doing all the work. Teddy keeps inspecting some ornaments and more of the presents under the tree.

"Aren't you going to open a present?" I ask.

"None of those are for me. They're for family and friends. I always send out presents two days after Christmas to my parents. They're retired in Arizona now," she says.

I play with her fingers, then the pre-wrapped present I got for her. She looks at it, then at me. I shrug. "I wanted to get you something. We're dating."

"Oh ..." I grab my bag and show Teddy a treat I got him. He loses his mind and chases it when I throw it. I shrug. "Both of you deserve a present."

She undoes the bow, then peels back the paper. She stares at the jewelry box and looks back at me. "How fast are we moving here, Hayden?"

"Not that fast, Molls. Calm your brain," I promise, kissing the top of her head.

She opens the box and there's a little gold 'present' locket. She stares at it for a long time. "Hayden, what is ..."

"You're my Christmas gift, I think. I mean, I came here expecting to hate the whole time, wanting to leave as soon as possible and now I don't want to go anywhere," I admit.

I feel so cheesy, so vulnerable and uncomfortable that I want to disappear. Molly pulls the necklace out, unclasps it and hands it to me. She holds her hair up. "Please put it on?"

I clasp it around the back of her neck and kiss her nape. She shivers. "You're doing way too much for me."

"I'm willing to do a lot more, babe. This is just the start. I'm going to be a wonderful boyfriend to you," I promise. "The distance won't matter. We'll barely feel it."

"You say that now, but you've gotten very used to having me in your bed every night," she says with a chuckle.

I groan. "Then no sex tonight. You have to wait until it's Christmas."

She laughs and snuggles closer to me. "I'm so glad we're together, Hayden. I ..."

"What?"

"I um.. wished upon a star for something like this. It was after I saw you at the bar, but the girls keep teasing me that you're my wish come true," she admits, her face flushing red.

I beam and pull her close, kissing her passionately. She moans as our hands wander, but I catch her hands. "Oh, no you don't. You don't get to use sweet lines against me."

"It's true, but I bet I could seduce you if I tried."

"You listen here," I warn her. "It might kill me, but I'll resist. I'll make it to midnight."

She laughs and hugs me tight. "We'll make it a lot longer than that, Hayden."

I grin, believing it. "I know we will, babe."

TEN

Molly

———

"Are you sure about telling them all at once?" I ask, fidgeting in the *limo* that picked us up from the airport. No matter how many private flights we'd taken over the year or how many times Hayden flashed his money around, I still haven't gotten used to it.

His hand slides over mine on my belly, and he kisses my temple. "It'll be easiest to tell them once, watch them get excited, show them the ultrasound, and then enjoy Christmas."

My belly doesn't look any different. I don't feel much different. It's hard to believe a baby is growing inside me. Hayden swears he can see it on the ultrasound, but I can't, not really. The doctor said that was normal since I'm only about two months along.

I take an unsteady breath. It's been our secret since I first thought it was possible when I was late. I nibble my bottom lip and Hayden turns my cheek to face him. "I thought you'd be happy to have me back in Mistletoe Meadows."

"Everything feels different," I say. "Before you were just visiting and now ..."

"Hell of a time to tell my parents about us, isn't it?" he asks with a smile. "Now that we know you're pregnant."

I feel my face blush. "Maybe we should test it on the girls first?"

"Let's. I'm in the mood for coffee. We can get you some decaf and some of those cookies you have been craving," he says.

Teddy whines and Hayden takes pity on him, freeing him from his crate. Teddy beelines it to me, pushing between my legs to sniff my belly before laying his head on my lap. Teddy gave us the first sign something was different. He doesn't want me getting up, wants to lay his head on my belly—something he's never done—and he stopped jumping on me altogether. He'll just whine around my feet now.

Hayden kisses me again. "Both of us are excited for the baby."

"No rushing, I still have, like … seven months to go," I tease.

"Good. seven months of me spoiling you, doting on you, figuring out how to be a good father," he says.

As we get to my place—Hayden carrying everything in—I watch him. He's done a complete flip since I showed him the positive tests. When we went to the doctor, the first time to confirm it, I'm pretty sure he got sick. The doctor said it was a panic attack, but he'd been unable to get his head around it.

He'd kept saying he couldn't do it, that he was barely boyfriend material, how could he be 'dad' material? Apparently, he's finding a way. I bundle tighter in my jacket and Teddy grabs the leash in his mouth, tugging me forward.

I get inside and find Hayden has already turned on the heat and the heated floors to war with the snow outside. It's thicker this year, feels colder. I get my shoes off, take off my jacket, then I'm in Hayden's arms again.

"No one knows we're here yet," he says with a mischievous

smile. "How about we get Teddy set up, then go have some fun in bed?"

"They don't know we're here?" I ask.

"I said we'd arrive at night and it's only three p.m. We have plenty of time to settle in, enjoy each other, watch the sunset." He wiggles his eyebrows. "I bet you can even find a scarf to tie me up with."

I giggle, but we follow through, giving Teddy his water and food, then hurrying upstairs like eager teenagers. Hayden strips me like it's a timed Olympic sport, and he's determined to take gold. The only thing he leaves on is the locket he got me last year for Christmas.

"I'm never going to get enough of you," he breathes.

"You say that every time," I murmur as I stroke over his sculpted body, following the lines of tattoo and muscle.

"I'll prove it. Look at that view," he says, turning me around as he sits on the bed.

The view is the last thing on my mind, but Hayden takes care of that before I can say a word, pulling me onto his lap and sliding inside me. I gasp as my back arches. I huff. "You tricked me."

"Watch the mountains you love while I fuck you senseless," he orders me.

He cups my breast in one hand and rubs my clit with the other as we move together. I wrap an arm around his neck and face him, kissing his neck, biting his ear, touching him and tasting him however I can.

A low groan leaves his throat. "Babe-"

"You're a better view," I argue, looking at his clenched jaw, his intense eyes, the flush in his cheeks. "I love you."

He blinks a few times, then forgets all about the mountains. He tosses me in bed and grinds inside of me hard and deep. His hands are gentle, but the light bites he litters on my skin, the way he loves me with no restraint, that's the Hayden I can't get enough of. He's like a drug and I need it.

He pushes me over the edge by rubbing my clit and sucking my nipple and doesn't bother pulling out when he finishes. We're far past that point. We hold each other, his cock still engorged, twitching inside me with after shocks of pleasure that shoot through me again and again.

He lays his head on my belly, rubbing my thighs. "So when are we going to feel kicking?"

I laugh and run my hand through his hair. "I thought you were worried about the baby."

"Now that I've got a good team of assistants and rarely need to be at the office and passed my title to another person in the chapter, I'm determined to be the dad I wanted," he says, taking my hand and kissing each of my fingertips.

"It'll be a while," I whisper. "Think you can settle for me until then?"

Hayden raises his face, then lies next to me, cuddling me close. "Being with you isn't 'settling', Molly. Every time you've come back here, or I've gone back to Miami and we've had to be apart, I was worried *you* would leave *me*. After that first time ... fuck, all I could think about was how much I missed you, wanted to be with you, wanted to tell you all the good and bad."

I feel my face heat and shake my head. "You say that like we've had a perfect year. Don't you remember the fights?"

"Fights mean we care about each other ... when they're not every day. We were fighting each other to make our relationship stronger," he kisses my nose. "Now I know better than to fight you."

"Is that so?" I kiss him with a giggle. "So I'll just be the default win?"

He shakes his head. "We'll fight the problem together."

He touches my belly again and kisses my temple. "Are you hungry? I'm hungry."

"You can go have a smoke if you want one, Hayden."

He shakes his head. "I'm finished with that. I told you

once we got the news—no more smoking. Not around the baby. It's a terrible habit."

I can't disagree. I don't want him getting sick because of it. I don't want less time with him. Hayden looks at me, then smiles and kisses my forehead. "I love you too, Molly."

"You ... you didn't have to say it! It just slipped out because you ..." I don't know how to take it back. I'd hoped he hadn't heard it or processed it since we were having sex.

"I've loved you for nearly a year. I've loved you since that tree lighting ceremony when I didn't want to look away from you, didn't crave a cigarette more than I craved your smile. Silly me, thought I had to get the timing right to tell you that," he chuckles.

He goes to his clothes, fishes around in his pants, and holds something behind his back. I narrow my eyes. He'd shown me some kinky toys, just like this. Hayden gets on the bed and looks away. "We're kind of out of order on this, and this isn't because of the baby, it's because of everything we've said while we've been lying here. Because we're right where we started and you are the only woman for me... will you marry me, Molly?"

He pulls out a ring, a beautiful ring. It's a square diamond with smaller diamonds around it. My eyes water and I point at him. "How dare you do this while I'm pregnant and can't help but cry!"

He laughs and takes my hand. "I will love you forever, Molly. You and our baby. I want us to have everything. We've done it the hard way. Let's do it the easy way now."

"Yes, of course I want to marry you! I love you," I exclaim.

He slides the ring on my finger and hugs me tight, kissing my temple, my cheek, my jaw, my nose, wherever he can reach. We end up going another round in bed before Hayden insists on giving me some proper food for a pregnant woman. We watch the sunset, then go to Angela's bakery.

I had my ring in my pocket and Hayden tells the girls–who are all there working on decorating–that we're pregnant. Tamsin drops something, then gazes at me. "No way!"

We laugh and Hayden shows the ultrasound, showing where the baby is as he glows with joy. I hug him as he chuckles, and Angela squeals, pointing at my ring. I flash it. "Oh, yeah, this is new."

"Very new," Hayden agrees. "About time I lock you down and stop other guys from staring at you."

"Oh my gosh! A baby and an engagement!" Charlotte squeals. "Don't tell me you're going to elope!"

I haven't even thought about a wedding. I look at my belly and Hayden rubs my shoulder. "We'll figure it out, baby."

Before we can get into all the details, my phone rings. My parents. I look at Hayden and he nods. We tell them to go to my place and he tells his parents the same thing. We get there first and I cook while snacking on the sweets we bought from the bakery. Hayden ends up helping me, his nervous energy throwing me off.

"Hey, if you're not ready for this," I say, trailing off.

"We're-"

They knock on the door and in a second, our parents are in the living room, talking and chatting, except for Hayden's father. I know he's talked to them every now and again, hasn't hidden that we're together, but our mothers are chatting like old friends and my dad is admiring the architecture.

Hayden takes my hand. "Are you ready for this?"

"As ready as I can be."

We start the opposite way with our parents. I tell them we're engaged and both our moms run over to look at my ring. My dad shakes Hayden's hand. "Be good to her. I know she wouldn't marry you if you weren't more than everyone thinks."

Hayden nods. "She makes me a better person, the man I want to be."

Once the excitement dies down enough and they're talking about how and when and where we're going to get married, Hayden clears his throat and holds out a bag. He got his own Christmas bag? And stuffed it with tissue paper and everything.

"I'm kind of new to this Christmas thing—in terms of liking it, but I think you four will like the presents inside this bag. There's one for each of you," he says.

Hayden wraps his arms around me and his dad pats Teddy's head as he waits his turn. My mom screams first, then looks at me. "Are you serious?"

Hayden can't hide his smile. "Very serious."

As we tell both sets of parents our news, I'm filled with emotion watching the joy and tears on their faces. When Hayden's stoic father cries looking at the ultrasound, I know how much this means to him.

All the questions start, but soft blubbering quiets the room. Hayden's dad stares at the photo, his face red, eyes watering, and he shakes his head. "I was so worried about you all the way in Miami doing a job you hate and ... this is the best thing you've ever made, son."

Hayden swallows the lump in his throat, then kisses my temple. "Molly's doing the hard part."

Hayden has shed the cold, closed-off persona he once had in Miami. Seeing him grinning ear to ear, one hand cradling my still flat belly, the other wrapped around me, he's no longer the ruthless businessman who couldn't be vulnerable. He's going to be an incredible father.

"I can't believe it! I'm going to be a grandma!" my mom yells.

After the chaos and celebrations die down, Hayden and I stand on my porch watching the softly falling snow blanket the mountains. I rest my head on his chest as he holds me under the starry sky.

"Just think- next Christmas there will be four of us," Hayden murmurs before tilting my chin up for a lingering kiss.

The nervousness and self-doubt he once had about relationships has transformed into unbridled happiness for our future together. As he walks me inside with promises of hot cocoa by the fire, I know we're ready for whatever comes next. With Hayden's fierce devotion and protective streak balanced by my stability and belief in him, we've become an unbreakable team.

No matter what worries or obstacles get thrown our way on this journey into marriage and parenthood, I'm certain our love can conquer them all. This feels like the perfect new beginning to our own family Christmas traditions.

It's the best possible start to Christmas, with the best man I could ever imagine. I kiss Hayden. "I love you."

"However many Christmases we get from here on out, I plan on cherishing every single one with you by my side as my wife," he vows, voice thick with devotion.